Published 1985 by Derrydale Books, distributed by Crown Publishers, Inc.
©Fernand Nathan 1983   Text Copyright © 1985 Joshua Morris, Inc.

Original story by Alain Grée, illustrated by Luis Camps
Translated by Linda B. Booth

Sammy the Squirrel

Frog Pond Friends

Derrydale Books, New York

"**S**ammy, can you get the children's balloon? It's caught in the branches of the old oak. . . ."

"Sammy, I promised to take home some pine cones. Could you gather a few for me?"

"Sammy, the kite tangled itself up in the top of the poplar tree. You climb so fast—could you untangle it?"

The good-hearted squirrel immediately shoots up into the leaves, skipping from branch to branch, to help this one and that one.

During the summer squirrels always store up food for the winter. But our friend has been too busy helping others, and now that it's cold Sammy still hasn't found a minute to put aside even the smallest mushroom or the tiniest hazelnut.

"What are you going to do?" moans his wife, finding empty cupboards. "You can't let our children go hungry!"

Maybe he could find some fruit under the fallen leaves blanketing the forest. After a long day of work, Sammy brings back only four walnuts three chestnuts, and two mossy mushrooms. This meal won't last very long.

"We want some more!" the children say, in tears. "We're hungry!" Sammy is very upset: no fruit, no seeds, no nuts grow in the winter. Where will he find food for his family?

Sammy hurries over to see Benjamin. His friend the beaver will surely pick some fruit for him in the branches of his house.

''You haven't got a chance,'' answers Benjamin from his window.

''Felix the fox nibbled every last little bit.''

''Then I'll go see Ricky—raccoons always have food hidden away in a corner,'' thought Sammy.

"It's true," Ricky tells him, lounging in a hammock. "This past year I did store acorns and berries, but during the summer I was having such a good time amusing myself that I completely forgot where I put them."

Disappointed, Sammy runs to Harry's cabin. But the hedgehog is already hibernating comfortably between two logs just like he does every winter. Frog Pond Friends won't see him again until spring.

"Don't wake me till spring!"

"Why don't you search in the tree hollows?" suggests Ollie the
owl above their heads. "Something tells me you'll find more
than plain seeds. . . ."

"Tree hollows? Why didn't I think of that?" Sammy scolds
himself. He goes right to work, inspecting every tree trunk in
the clearing. Night falls, and his little ones are still hungry. In
the very last tree he discovers a strange-looking bottle. "Good
work Sammy. You have found a treasure!"

There is a paper stuck in the bottle. Wally the woodpecker graciously extracts it with his long beak.

"It's a parchment written by Redbeard the Pirate on his way back from the West Indies. Wow! It's a treasure map!" A treasure? In a flash all of the Frog Pond Friends gather around the mysterious drawing.

"Finding the hiding place will be easy with a map this good," boasts Ricky. "Get going, Sammy. We'll read the instructions—you follow the trail."

The squirrel climbs to the top of the cherry tree, leaps onto the blue cedar, counts four trees, then goes to the very top of the oak tree.

"Go down four branches, then onto the fallen trunk. . . ."

"Go four steps north," continues Ricky,
"as far as the great red pine."

"A pirate's chest is tied between the seventh and eighth branches."

"I found it!" shouts Sammy.

Ricky and Benjamin help him get the box down, and Benjamin's tools make fast work of the old padlock. Now the most delicious spectacle appears before the amazed group.

Blackberries from Jamaica! Pineapple from Guadeloupe! Blueberries from Trinidad! What wonderful jams and preserves, and plenty to last through two or three winters!

Sammy's story reminds us not to get discouraged. If we work hard, our good efforts will be rewarded one day. Happy days, squirrel family!

Till we meet again, Frog Pond Friends!

SQUIRRELS
MORE ABOUT THEM

Graceful, amusing, untiring, squirrels are always busy. They
live in the woods, and their diet includes bark, mushrooms,
berries, nuts, and pine cones.
In autumn they hoard food and hide it in a secret place:
under dead leaves, or in a hollow tree.

They will need their private store of food during the winter. Squirrel families live in nests made of twigs and moss. They build their nests on the high branches of a tree to protect against their most-feared enemies, the weasels and the marten.

The male guards the nest ferociously against buzzards and
vultures especially in the spring when mother squirrel gives
birth to her young.
Squirrels use their agility and speedy climbing to escape
from enemies. They leap from branch to branch as
gracefully as trapeze artists. Squirrels are capable of jumping
over fifteen feet in a single bound!

Good luck, squirrel friends !

Printed in Spain